SILVER PENNY STORIES

Cinderella

Told by Deanna McFadden

Illustrated by Valerie Sokolova

O nce upon a time, there was a sweet girl who was very young when her mother died. Soon after, the girl's father married a woman with two daughters of her own. After only a few years, the girl's father became ill and died.

The woman and her very selfish daughters were cruel, and the girl's father was no longer there to protect her.

They took her pretty clothes for themselves, made her do all the chores, and forced her to sleep by the fire. The cinders from the fire made her dusty and dirty. So they called her Cinderella.

Then one day, the house was bustling with excitement. The entire kingdom was invited to a grand ball in honor of the prince. He was looking for a bride.

Cinderella's stepsisters wanted to look their very best. They each wanted to marry the prince. They raced upstairs to their bedrooms to look through their wardrobes and jewelry boxes. Then they ordered Cinderella to help them get ready for the ball.

"Cinderella," they demanded, "mend our dresses and fix our hair!"

Cinderella turned to her stepmother, "May I go to the ball?"

Her stepmother laughed. "No, you have too many chores. You must wash the floors, dust all the furniture, and clean the whole house."

Cinderella got right to work. She scrubbed the floors and dusted all the furniture. Then she tidied the whole house.

"Cinderella! Cinderella!" her stepsisters called.

"Sew this ribbon on my dress right now," said the older one.

"Braid these ribbons in my hair," said the younger one.

And then it was time to leave. Again, Cinderella asked if she could go to the ball.

"No," her stepmother replied. "You have nothing to wear and you are simply too dirty."

Cinderella ran outside to the garden and began to cry.

Suddenly, a beautiful fairy godmother appeared. Cinderella was frightened.

"Don't be afraid," said the fairy godmother. "I am here to help. Do you wish to go to the ball?"

"Yes," said Cinderella, "but I have nothing to wear."

"Close your eyes," her fairy godmother said. She touched Cinderella on the shoulder with her magic wand.

When Cinderella opened her eyes, she was wearing the most beautiful dress in the world. It was spun with golden thread and decorated with silver pearls. On her feet she now wore a pair of delicate glass slippers.

"Now," her fairy godmother said, "I will need a pumpkin and some mice."

Cinderella fetched a pumpkin from the garden and six mice from the kitchen. The fairy godmother waved her magic wand. Suddenly, the pumpkin turned into a grand coach, and the mice turned into six strong horses.

"Oh, my!" Cinderella said. "How will I ever thank you?"

Her fairy godmother smiled and said, "Do not stay at the ball past midnight, for when the clock strikes twelve, everything will be as it was before."

Cinderella promised to be home in time.

Cinderella's coach raced to the ball. When Cinderella entered the palace, no one recognized her. She was so enchanting, the prince could not take his eyes off her. He danced with her all evening.

Suddenly the clock chimed. It was almost midnight! Cinderella had to leave before the magic spell broke. When the prince turned away for a moment, Cinderella ran out of the hall and down the palace steps. She ran so quickly, one of the glass slippers fell off her foot.

Just as the clock struck twelve, Cinderella arrived home. The coach turned back into a pumpkin, the horses turned back into mice, and Cinderella's clothes were tattered and dirty again.

When her stepmother and stepsisters returned, Cinderella was asleep by the fire, wearing her dusty old clothes.

At the palace, the prince found Cinderella's glass slipper. Desperate to see the enchanting maiden again, he took it to the king.

"The young woman whose foot fits this slipper shall be my bride," he said.

The news spread across the kingdom. The stepsisters giggled with excitement when the prince arrived at the door. He had visited every house in the land, and the slipper had not fit anyone.

Cinderella's two stepsisters sat down to try on the beautiful glass slipper. The older stepsister's feet were too long.

"She is not the one," the prince said.

The younger stepsister's feet were too wide.

"Nor is she," he said.

"Is there another young woman in this house?" the prince asked Cinderella's stepmother.

"Only Cinderella, but she didn't go to the ball," she said.

"Fetch her," the prince ordered.

Cinderella sat down in front of the prince, and the shoe slipped easily onto her pretty little foot.

"I knew it was you!" he said, beaming.

Then he took her hand gently and helped her to his beautiful carriage. Cinderella and the prince rode away, leaving Cinderella's stepmother and stepsisters behind.

The kingdom rejoiced at the marriage, and Cinderella and the prince lived happily ever after.